The Little Yellow Digger
Saves Christmas

Written by Peter Gilderdale
Illustrated by Fifi Colston

Based on the characters by Betty & Alan Gilderdale

SCHOLASTIC
AUCKLAND SYDNEY NEW YORK LONDON TORONTO
MEXICO CITY NEW DELHI HONG KONG

There was just one day till Christmas,
we were setting up our play.
The phone rang. It was Santa!
And we all heard him say . . .

"I'm driving to your school play,
but I've had some awful luck.
The mountainside came tumbling down
and swallowed up my truck.
I'm sorry, I can't get to you.
I am completely STUCK."

"Oh no!" the grownups cried aloud.
"Whatever will we do?
It really isn't Christmas
if Santa's not here too!"

We said, "That isn't Santa!
He wouldn't stay away,
because he would be flying
in his special Christmas sleigh."

But Santa heard, and told us,
"I'm only in this truck
because my reindeer caught a cold,
so into bed they're tucked!"

"Poor Rudolf is embarrassed,
won't let himself be seen.
You cannot lead the reindeer
when your nose is glowing green!"

"So now you know," said Santa.
"It's all out of control.
This Christmas I have simply had
to *drive* from the North Pole!
But I can't make deliveries when
the truck's been swallowed whole."

So how could we have Christmas
with Santa stuck that way?
And who would hand out presents
to finish off our play?
It looked like Christmas Eve would be
a disappointing day!

But . . .
the little yellow digger
was in our parking bay.
The digger driver's daughter
was helping with our play.

"Our digger can save Santa!"
the driver's daughter said.
"It's sitting doing nothing.
It can clear the road instead!"

The digger rumbled up the road
and we all followed too.
We drove off in a convoy
that grew and grew and grew.

But when we got there – what a mess!
The road was full of muck.
The mud had swallowed Santa
and his bright red Christmas truck.
Poor Santa and the presents.
They were all completely STUCK!

The digger started digging.
It dug, and dug, and dug!
And then it pulled the truck out
with a gloopy, gloppy glug.

The truck was full of muddy goo,
The engine wouldn't go.
And we began to worry
Santa wouldn't see our show.

For Santa simply stood there,
a sad and sorry figure.
But then he had a good idea ...
he'd drive the little digger!

It led the convoy back to school,
and Santa loved our play,
but after handing presents out,
he said he couldn't stay.

"I have a busy night ahead.
My job has got much bigger.
Yet I can still save Christmas
if I drive the little digger!"

Then Santa took the digger
and drove off on his way
to go deliver presents
so boys and girls could play.

And that is how the digger
came to help out Santa Claus.
It's why we think that it deserves
a round of loud applause.

And if on Christmas Eve you hear
a rumbling that gets bigger . . .
just maybe it is Santa
on the Little Yellow Digger.

For Jaylen, Liliana and Theodore – P.G.

For our boy Rory, who would fall asleep with the original book in
his arms when he was just a little digger – F.C.

First published in 2020 by Scholastic New Zealand Limited
Private Bag 94407, Botany, Auckland 2163, New Zealand

Scholastic Australia Pty Limited
PO Box 579, Gosford, NSW 2250, Australia

Text © Peter Gilderdale, 2020
Illustrations © Fifi Colston, 2020

The moral rights of the author and illustrator have been asserted.

ISBN 978-1-77543-623-2

A catalogue record for this book is available from the National Library of New Zealand.

12 11 10 9 8 7 6 5 4 3 2 1   0 1 2 3 4 5 6 7 8 9 / 2

Illustrations created in gouache on watercolour paper.

Publishing team: Lynette Evans, Penny Scown and Abby Haverkamp
Designer: Leon Mackie
Typeset in Skolar Latin
Printed in China by RR Donnelley

Scholastic New Zealand's policy is to use papers that are renewable and made efficiently from wood grown in responsibly managed forests,
so as to minimise its environmental footprint.